VINTAGE S.F.
in the Popular Magazines:
A Checklist 1874-1936

By Igor Spajic

Cover Design by Mark Nelson
(www.southfarmdesign)

S.F. Heritage Press No.2

Copyright © 2017 Igor Spajic

All rights reserved.

ISBN: 978-0-6487522-1-9

CONTENTS

Before SF Had a Home

Science fiction was published in fiction magazines before it ever had a name. The term 'scientific romance' was used in the Victorian era to mean not some love interest, but a flight of imagination based on some scientific idea or knowledge.

The 1890s saw a boom in popular fiction magazines, as increasing numbers of people were literate and looking for inexpensive entertainment. There was the choice of playing the piano at home (and singing along), going to the theatre or to the cheaper music hall. And then there was reading.

The paragon of popular fiction was *The Argosy*, an all fiction magazine published by Frank Munsey from 1888 onwards. Besides providing straight adventure, romance and mystery stories, *The Argosy* and its stablemates *All-Story Weekly* and *The Cavalier* (and their rivals from other publishers) also ran fantasy, detective, horror and of course, science fiction. Their heyday was the early 20th century before World War I.

These magazines were broadly separated into two categories: the 'pulps' and the 'slicks'. The former were printed on cheaper, pulp paper, sometimes scarcely better than found in newspapers. The paper was matte, slightly brown in colour and the magazine edges went untrimmed. Covers were bright and colourful and did not skimp on promoting the contents, either with a dramatic illustration and/or a highlight of some popular author or story series.

Apart from the general fiction titles, a plethora of niche pulps erupted, covering genres such as detective/crime, westerns, air combat, romance, western romances, G-Men, Hollywood stories, racy night life, jungle adventures and sometimes strange combinations of these.

The 'slicks' on the other hand cost more and had more of a quality image, thanks to their neatly trimmed edges and glossy, white paper. Their editorial standards were usually higher as well, demanding thoughtful articles and well-written stories that could at least have some claim as 'literature' rather than just fiction.

But SF was not yet named, nor yet had a home. It was a vagabond, appearing occasionally in a range of general interest or niche magazines.

The point of the list in *Vintage Science Fiction in the Popular Magazines: A Checklist 1874-1936* is to document those SF stories that have appeared in the general or non-SF publications. This requires detective work and a knowledge of the magazines of the period.

Some of the science-oriented stories from this time might be classified today as fantasy rather than strict SF. The divisions between these genres were not so definite back then, and much science fiction was pervaded with a sense of wonder and mystery, less of the hard nuts and bolts approach we would recognise today.

Even after science-fiction-only magazines were established, SF continued to appear in the popular fiction magazines. There were three principal reasons: first, the general fiction magazines' circulations were higher than SF-only titles and so an author's work received more exposure; second, the readers of these magazines expected the occasional science-laced story; and third, they paid the authors much better rates than the SF magazines.

By 1930, there were already six SF magazines, including two quarterly editions. The rigours of the Great Depression weakened their publishers but the basic titles continued under new ownership. By 1939, there was a second boom in SF pulp magazines as a dozen new titles appeared over the following two years. Most disappeared just as quickly after failing to find a readership that would sustain them. Many later succumbed to wartime rationing of paper and other shortages.

From here onwards, SF finally began to disappear from the general fiction titles. But conversely, the era of the pulps themselves was virtually over. The world had changed. First, the cinema and then the radio challenged the pulp magazines as inexpensive entertainment. Then after World War II, the cheap paperback book began to flood the reading market, taking customers away from fiction magazines. (Not to mention the advent of television, that new monopoliser of people's leisure time!)

One by one the magazines folded, with specialty titles catering to detective and science fiction persisting longest, into the mid-1950s.

Surviving SF magazines shrank to the digest size (in imitation of the paperback format) and held their modest readership. Some are still with us today.

Acknowledgments

The bulk of this listing originates from the diligent work of Julius Schwartz in the *Fantasy Magazine* (also titled as *Science Fiction Digest*), which was among the first SF fan magazines in the 1930s. Contributions to the lists were also made by Isadore Manzon, Donald Wollheim, Raymond A. Palmer and Henry Hasse. I am indebted to these SF fans (before they became pros in the field) who represent the first generation of SF enthusiasts.

I am also grateful for the scholarship and insights of writers about SF, such as Brian Aldiss, Mike Ashley, Sam Moskowitz, etc. whose books grace my shelves.

My gratitude also extends to the webmasters of The Internet Speculative Fiction Database at:

http://www.isfdb.org/cgi-bin/pl.cgi?589198

which I found invaluable in checking and correcting the many errors that creep into compilations of lists from a variety of people.

What's Listed

In order to keep this book a reasonable size, the scope has been necessarily limited. The listing is for American magazine titles only, though a few British ones from the 19th and early 20th Centuries are also included.

Specifically excluded from this book are, of course, stories appearing in the science fiction magazines themselves (which would make a truly enormous project) and also excluded are the science magazines that published occasional SF.

One other exclusion of note is *Weird Tales*, a pulp magazine somewhat in a category of its own. Justly subtitled 'The Unique Magazine', *Weird Tales* featured fantasy, horror and 'weird' stories but also much SF, especially throughout the 1920s. It served to introduce the work of H. P. Lovecraft (the Cthulhu mythos), Robert E. Howard (*Conan the Barbarian*) and other writers whose work has since reached cult popularity status. The science fiction content of *Weird Tales* was so consistent (at least in the period covered by this book) that it should be (and often has been) included among the SF-only titles.

Where to Find these Stories

You, the reader, may ask 'What's the point of this list if it doesn't help me find interesting SF that I haven't read before?' In answer, here's a beginning to finding your way to some excellently written and imaginative science fiction.

Online Archives

University of New Zealand – Periodicals, Books and Authors – found at:

http://www.unz.org/Pub/

this is the University of New Zealand's web archive. An excellent source of titles and issues with whole magazines reproduced (in PDF) in some cases, and with fiction available that is in the public domain.

Many novels and novelettes as well as short stories from the pre-SF magazines were reprinted in later pulp publications that catered specially for contemporary readers (in the 1940s) who had perhaps heard of but never found the classic older stories. The premier reprint magazines were *Fantastic Novels* and *Famous Fantastic Mysteries*, later merged together due to wartime rationing. Within their pages the old classics appeared again, such as *The Moon Pool* and *The Face in the Abyss*, both by A. Merritt and Ray Cummings' *The Girl in the Golden Atom*. This time, they were beautifully illustrated by Virgil Finlay, whose work has attracted just praise for its technique and painstaking textures.

These reprint magazines can be found at the Archive and most issues have been reproduced. They are an excellent source of fantasy and SF from the pre-1935 era.

Project Gutenberg - An excellent place to find certain novels and novelettes is Project Gutenberg at:

www.gutenberg.org

Project Gutenberg aims to scan and make available books and magazines that are in the public domain. These are made available in a number of different formats. Searches through the database can be made using author's name or story title.

Google Books – titles in the public domain have been scanned from original books held in public libraries and archives. Other books not in the public domain have been copied as well and there is an ongoing controversy regarding this with copyright holders. You can start your search here:

https://archive.org/details/googlebooks?&sort=-downloads&page=2

Some quite rare and obscure books have been scanned but beware! Google books are often poorly scanned documents: pages may be missing and the illustrations (if any) have not been scanned to best advantage.

The Internet Archive – If you search by magazine title, you will find many issues on the Internet Archive. For example,

https://archive.org/details/AllStoryWeeklyV069N0219170324

will bring you to the archive of *All-Story Weekly* magazines. Individual collections within the Archive will provide more coverage.

The Pulp Magazine Archive – found at:

https://archive.org/details/pulpmagazinearchive

Though at the moment (2017), coverage is spotty, with some titles featured much more than others, new titles are being added. An excellent source for certain science fiction magazines, scanned into several digital formats.

Paperback reprints – many fantasy and SF titles from before WWII were re-issued shortly after it in the first generations of paperbacks. Some such books may be pricey due to rarity or special interest though most would be available at modest prices.

1950s paperbacks have an appearance of their own in terms of the cover art, which can be quite stylised or have a pulp-like 'action' flavour. Many classic SF titles have also been reprinted in the 1960s by Ace Books.

Copies of these paperbacks are available through second-hand book dealers or through Amazon or E-Bay. Search for them by book title or by an author's name if his/her work piques your interest. Most such copies will be inexpensive to buy or ship.

Hardback reprints – typically, after a serialisation in a fiction magazine a novel would find publication as a hardback book. Such first editions are highly collectible and this reflects their asking prices. Subsequent editions may cost less, but hardbacks are better bound, using a higher grade of paper, and so are more prized than paperbacks.

They are also larger and heavier than paperbacks and will cost more to ship. Most hardbacks are probably missing their dust jackets, those colourful paper wrappers that tore easily. A number of enterprising companies are offering high-quality reproductions of dust jackets of specific titles and editions for a modest fee. These can dress up the often plain hardback cover into something striking and as good as new.

Again, consult second-hand book dealers or go to E-Bay or Amazon.

Specific Collections in state or university libraries – such collections as have been gathered by one collector over a lifetime might be bequeathed to an institution of learning as part of the collector's last will and testament. Other collections may have been put together through the diligence and searching of a number of interested people.

Some of these collections might have been scanned and digitised and be available online (see UNZ above), but most would only be available to examine and read in person. The more precious books and magazines may not be available for borrowing at all and only be read within the library itself.

Collectors' Markets – Become a collector of pulp magazines and buy/sell through collectors' markets. Dedicated collectors often issue lists of items they have to sell and want ads for that last issue of *Doc Savage* to complete a set. Read the forums and become familiar with asking/selling prices. If you deal with people recognised in this community, you won't be ripped off.

Once you have a set of original pulp magazines (whether SF or some other genre), these issues will keep their value – at least amongst other collectors. First issues or issues featuring the first published appearances of a famous author are worth more than other numbers of the magazine, and complete collections of every issue, or sets covering an entire year also command a premium.

As mentioned above, the reprint magazines *Fantastic Novels* and *Famous Fantastic Mysteries* from the 1940s and early 1950s are an excellent source for earlier SF and fantasy. They reflect prices for pulp magazines of that era, which are considerably less than for issues of *The Argosy* and *All-Story Weekly* from the 1910s and 1920s. They are also more easily found, having perhaps a better survival rate. It's a lot more satisfying to have such magazines rather than a scanned PDF document version downloaded from the net which you might, at best, print out in a facsimile of the real thing.

Store your magazines responsibly in acid-proof plastic sleeves and in cool, dry places out of direct sunlight. The sleeves protect against abrasion damaging the covers further, while sunlight must be kept at bay or it will fade any printed colours. Comic book emporiums might be the easiest way to purchase such acid-proof sleeves as they use them widely to protect comics, which were historically also printed on the cheaper pulp paper.

Be careful with the edges of the magazine cover as they may be a bit frayed or with small tears. Prevent the tears from getting larger with a sparing use of clear magic tape on the inside of the cover. Just snip little sections of tape for individual tears. DO NOT use plain cellotape – it will yellow and even brown with age and leave stains on the paper after it's fallen off. With any tape, take extreme care. Work on a clean tabletop with plenty of light. If misapplied, it's hard to lift the tape off again without tearing up what you were trying to save.

Dampness of course, is harmful to any printed paper but particularly to pulp paper, which carries within itself the seeds of its own destruction. This is an acid component that gradually browns the paper, while it also becomes increasingly brittle and easy to tear. Dampness will accelerate this effect. Moisture will also grow mould, so keep your collection dry!

Museum conservators have a technique for preserving rare or precious books printed on pulp-like paper: they undo the binding and soak the publication—sheet by sheet—in a special alkaline solution. The wet sheets are then allowed to dry under controlled conditions. The acid content is forever removed and once dry and carefully rebound, the document will suffer no more degradation over time, even over extreme lengths of time. Needless to say, this mustn't be even attempted unless you know exactly what you're doing. And the paid cost in labour of this operation ensures it is usually reserved for very special documents.

Unlike the pulps, the 'slicks' with their shiny, better grade of paper don't have this weakness, but must still be kept in cool, dry, dark storage. Use repellents in the room to stop damage by silverfish or other insects.

As a collector, you're the custodian of a rare treasure—the popular entertainment of a century ago. Cheap and lurid some of the pulp magazines may have been, and so not especially valued when new. Many copies were thrown away after being read and are thus quite rare nowadays. Treat them carefully so that you too can bequeath them to posterity.

Guide to Magazine Titles

Here's a sample of the publications which published the most SF content. The Munsey group lead in that regard, but some magazines merged with others in that publisher's stable and names were changed to reflect this.

The Argosy, a Munsey publication (starting out as a children's magazine *The Golden Argosy*) became a fiction magazine for adults on Dec. 1, 1888 first as a weekly, becoming in turn a monthly from April 1894 to Sept. 1917, when it became a weekly again, until 17 July 1920, after which it merged with *All-Story Weekly* for 7 Aug. 1920 to become *Argosy-All-Story Weekly*.

All-Story Magazine, a Munsey publication, began in Jan. 1905 as a monthly, becoming a weekly from 7 Mar. 1914 to its 7 Aug. 1920 merger with *The Argosy*. In between, from 16 May 1914 to 8 May, 1915 *All-Story* absorbed *The Cavalier* to become *All-Story Cavalier Weekly*.

Argosy-All-Story Weekly, a Munsey publication, began from the merger between *The Argosy* and *All-Story Weekly* (see above) on 7 Aug. 1920, lasting until 28 Sept. 1929. Afterwards, the title was changed to simply *Argosy*, retaining its weekly schedule.

The Blue Book, a Story-Press Corporation and Consolidated Magazines publication, first came out as *Monthly Story Magazine* from May 1905 to Aug. 1906, then *Monthly Story Blue Book Magazine* on Sept. 1906–April 1907, followed by minor variations on the *Blue Book* name until 1975. It was sold to McCall Publications in 1929.

The Cavalier, a Munsey publication, began on October 1908 and merged with *The Scrap Book* (see below) on Jan. 6, 1912, before merging again with *All-Story* after its May 9, 1914 issue to become *All-Story Cavalier Weekly* until the *Cavalier* reference was dropped after May 8, 1915.

The Cosmopolitan Magazine, was first published in 1886 as a family-oriented magazine, changing hands after a couple of years before being acquired by Hearst Magazines in 1905. It was transformed into a literary magazine which published works by Jack London, O. Henry, George Bernard Shaw and Upton Sinclair.

It was merged with *Hearst's International* magazine in 1925 but was titled simply as *Cosmopolitan*. Through most of the 1930s, *Cosmopolitan* achieved a circulation of 1,700,000 and sold a popular blend of fiction, non-fiction articles, and special features. Circulation dropped through the 1950s until it was completely remodelled as a woman's magazine in 1965 by new editor Helen Gurley Brown.

Everybody's Magazine, beginning in Sept. 1899, imported much content from the British publisher Pearson Publishing's magazines, before sourcing home-grown material. *Everybody's* was a 'slick' magazine before becoming a pulp in 1927. It combined with The Ridgway Company's *Romance* after the Mar. 1929 issue.

Flynn's Detective Weekly, came out on Sept. 20, 1924 as *Flynn's*, becoming *Flynn's Weekly* in 1926 to underscore the point. Red Star News Company published the title, which became ever more focussed on the detective genre, declaring itself as *Flynn's Weekly Detective Fiction* in 1927, *Detective Fiction Weekly* in 1928, just *Detective Fiction* in 1941 (it had become fortnightly), *Flynn's Detective* in 1942 (now under the Frank A. Munsey Company), *Flynn's Detective Fiction* in 1943-4 (under Popular Publications), before ceasing due to wartime conditions. A 1951 reappearance as plain *Detective Fiction*, was also under the Popular Publications banner, but the magazine found no readership and petered out after six issues that year.

Oriental Stories, published from Oct. 1930 to Jan. 1934, was retitled *Magic Carpet* from Jan. 1933. There was a total of 14 issues, which included some fantasy, horror and SF.

The Popular Magazine, from Street & Smith Publications, spanned Dec. 1903 through Sep. 1927, (briefly afterwards until Oct 1928 as *Popular Stories* before returning to the original title) through Oct. 1931 then merging with *Complete Stories*. It was always on a monthly schedule.

Pearson's Magazine, was an English title first published in Jan. 1896 by C. Arthur Pearson, who also served as the first editor. An imitator of *The Strand* magazine, Pearson's focussed more heavily on romance and adventure, showcasing the works of Rudyard Kipling, H. G. Wells, Baroness Orczy, and C. J. Cutcliffe Hyne. *Pearson's* last issue was Nov. 1939, by which we can presume that it was killed off by British wartime paper rationing. A parallel version published in U.S.A. began in Mar. 1899 as a straight reprint of the British editions, before sourcing more and more local stories and content. The American *Pearson's Magazine* lasted into 1925.

The Scrap Book, a Munsey publication, debuted in Mar. 1906 and maintained a monthly schedule through Jan. 1912, after which it merged with *The Cavalier* (see above).

Short Stories, a Street & Smith publication, commenced in June 1890 and shifted focus from general to adventure fiction in 1910, when it was taken over by Doubleday, Page & Co. Always a monthly, *Short Stories* continued into 1959, when it was briefly retitled as *Short Stories for Men* for its last five issues, ending in August 1959.

The Strand Magazine, published from Jan. 1891 through Oct. 1949 was Britain's most popular fiction magazine, and maintained a loyal readership through publishing series stories, which followed the adventures of the same characters. The most famous example of this were the Sherlock Holmes tales of Arthur Conan Doyle. Other famous writers included W. W. Jacobs, H. G. Wells, Rudyard Kipling, Anthony Hope, O. Henry, and P. G. Wodehouse.

Thrilling Adventures was published from Dec. 1931 through Nov. 1943 on a monthly basis, but skipped issues in its last year due to wartime shortages.

Top-Notch, began as *Top-Notch Magazine* on Mar. 1910 as a monthly, becoming fortnightly at the end of the year as *Top-Notch*. The '*Magazine*' returned in the title, but the schedule remained through April 1, 1931, after which it was sold to Street & Smith Publications, and re-titled *Street & Smith's Top-Notch Magazine*, keeping the fortnightly schedule until Nov. 1932, after which it became a monthly until 1937, when it combined a couple of issues to struggle into Sep./Oct. which became its last.

The list below contains publication issue date, story title, author(s) and magazine title. The number listed after the magazine title indicates in how many parts a serial ran.

ISSUE	TITLE	AUTHOR(S)	MAGAZINE
1874			
May	The Mysterious Island	Jules Verne	Scribner's Magazine 11
1876			
Jan. 1	Journey into the Unknown	Julian Hawthorne	Appleton's Magazine
1889			
Nov. 16	The Conquest of the Moon	André Laurie	The Argosy
1890			
Apr.	The Appendicula Vermiformis	Arthur Hardy	Cosmopolitan Magazine
1895			
Feb.	The Purple Death	W. L. Alden	Cassell's Magazine
1896			
Dec.	The Purple Pileus	H. G. Wells	Black and White
1897			
May	The War of the Worlds	H. G. Wells	Cosmopolitan Magazine 8
Nov.	The Microbe of Death	Rudolph de Cordova	Pearson's Magazine
1898			
Jan. 12	Edison's Conquest of Mars	Garrett P. Serviss	New York Journal (newspaper) 5
Feb.	London's Danger	C. J. Cutcliffe Hyne	Pearson's Magazine
Feb.	The Lizard	C. J. Cutcliffe Hyne	The Strand Magazine
Feb. 5	The Empress of the Earth	M. P. Shiel	Short Stories 18
1899			
July	The Lost Continent	C. J. Cutcliffe Hyne	Pearson's Magazine 5
Aug.	Stories of the Sanctuary Club	Mead & Eustace	The Strand Magazine
Aug.	The Monster of Lake LaMetrie	Wardon Allan Curtis	Pearson's Magazine
Sept.	The Master of the Octopus	Edward Olin Weeks	Pearson's Magazine
Sept.	The Purple Terror	Fred M. White	The Strand Magazine

ISSUE	TITLE	AUTHOR(S)	MAGAZINE
1899			
Nov.	The Wheels of Dr. Ginochio Gyves	Ellsworth Douglass & Edwin Pallander	Cassell's Magazine
Dec. 16	Man: Ages Hence	Anonymous	Evening Post
1900			
Jan.	Honeymoon in Space (Stories of Other Worlds)	George Griffith	Pearson's Magazine 6
Jan.	Nature's Next Move	Barry Pain	Pearson's Magazine 5
Apr.	Within an Ace of the End of the World	Robert Barr	MacClure's Magazine
Nov.	The First Men in the Moon	H. G. Wells	Cosmopolitan Magazine 8
1901			
Feb.	The Man Who Meddled with Eternity	E. Tickner-Edwards	The Harmsworth Magazine
Feb.	The Raid of Le Vengeur	George Griffith	Pearson's Magazine
Jun.	The Lady Automaton	E. E. Kellett	Pearson's Magazine
Jul.	The Last Days of Earth	George C. Wallis	The Harmsworth Magazine
Dec.	The Thames Valley Catastrophe	Grant Allen	The Strand Magazine
Dec.	The Last Stand of the Decapods	Frank T. Bullen	The Strand Magazine
Dec.	The Professor's Experiment	Elizabeth M. Rhodes	The Argosy
Dec.	A Corner in Cats	Mary E. Stickney	The Argosy
1902			
Mar.	The Dupe of a Realist	J. George Frederick	The Argosy
Mar.	Silas Ricker's Magno Thermometer	William F. Brown	The Argosy
1903			
Jan.	The Four White Days	Fred M. White	Pearson's Magazine
Jan.	Dr. Cox's Discovery	Herbert Wood	Cosmopolitan Magazine
Feb.	The Black Shadow	Owen Oliver	Cassell's Magazine
Feb.	The Four Days' Night	Fred M. White	Pearson's Magazine
Mar.	The Dust of Death	Fred M. White	Pearson's Magazine
May	The End of the World	Simon Newcomb	MacClure's Magazine
Jun.	The Invisible Force	Fred M. White	Pearson's Magazine
Sep.	The Hawkins Pumpless Pump	Edgar Franklin	The Argosy

ISSUE	TITLE	AUTHOR(S)	MAGAZINE
1903			
Nov.	The Food of the Gods	H. G. Wells	Cosmopolitan Magazine 10
Dec.	The Elixir of Life	C. Langton Clarke	The Argosy
Dec.	The Hawkins Anti-Fire Fly	Edgar Franklin	The Argosy
1904			
Jan.	In the Interest of Science	Oscar H. Hawley	The Argosy
Jan.	The Hawkins Crook-Trap	Edgar Franklin	The Argosy
Feb.	At Jupiter's Call	H. F. Farnham	The Popular Magazine
Mar.	The Curious Case of Thomas Dunbar	G. M. Barrows	The Argosy
Mar.	Mr. Casey's Negotiable Stomach	Colin K. Colin	The Argosy
Aug.	The Power Behind a Throne	William F. Brown	The Argosy
Aug.	The Blue Peter Troglodyte	William Wallace Cook	The Argosy
Sept.	A Star Fell	L. J. Beeston	Cassell's Magazine
Oct.	The Green Spider	A. Sarsfield Ward	Pearson's Magazine
Oct.	From Pole to Pole	George Griffith	The Windsor Magazine
Nov.	The Great White Moth	Fred M. White	The Strand Magazine
1905			
Jan.	When Time Slipped a Cog	W. Bert Foster	The All-Story Magazine
Feb.	The Golden Flood	Edwin Lefevre	MacClure's Mag. 4
Apr.	From the Deep Sea	Henry C. Rowland	The Popular Magazine 2
May	Mr. 'iggins' Invisible Cloth	E. J. Appleton	The Popular Magazine
May	The Moon Metal	Garrett P. Serviss	The All-Story Magazine
Sep.	The Peculiar Cruise of the Tortoise	Ralph T. Yates	The Argosy
Sep.	The Time Reflector	George Allan England	Monthly Story Magazine
Nov.	With the Night Mail	Rudyard Kipling	MacClure's Magazine

The All-Story, June 1909

"The Hawkins Improved Diving-Bell" by Edgar Franklin, *The Argosy*, Sept. 1910

ISSUE	TITLE	AUTHOR(S)	MAGAZINE
1906			
Jan.	The Man from Atlantis	A. H. Sill	Overland Magazine
Jan.	In the Days of the Comet	H. G. Wells	Cosmopolitan Magazine 8
Feb.	The Monster Flea	E. J. Knight-Adkin	Pearson's Magazine 5
Feb.	The Sound Machine	E. J. Appleton	The Popular Magazine
Mar.	Forty-One Nights of Mystery	Guy C. Hazzard	The Argosy
Mar.	Professor Jonkin and his Busier Bees	Howard Garis	The Argosy
May	A Gift from Mars	W. W. Cook	The Argosy 5
May	The Man in the Air	Frederick L. Keates	The Scrap Book
Jul.	Bagley's Automatic Grass-Hopper	Howard D. Smiley	The All-Story Magazine
Aug.	The Lunar Advertising Co. Ltd.	George Allan England	The Grey Goose
Aug.	The Shadow and the Flash	Jack London	The Windsor Magazine
Sep.	Land of Nowhere	G. E. Vincent	Chataquan Magazine

ISSUE	TITLE	AUTHOR(S)	MAGAZINE
1906			
Nov.	The Eighth Wonder	William Wallace Cook	The Argosy 4
1907			
Feb.	Bagley's Rain Machine	Howard D. Smiley	The Argosy
Apr.	The Sky Pirate	Garrett P. Serviss	The Scrap Book 6
Apr.	A Message from the Moon: The Story of a Great Coup	George Allan England	Pearson's Magazine
1908			
May	The Scourge of the World	H. A. & G. A. Thompson	The Live Wire
May	The War in the Air	H. G. Wells	Pearson's Magazine
Jul.	The Burning Image	Crittendon Marriott	The Live Wire 6
Aug.	The White Spot	Fred M. White	Pearson's Magazine
Sep.	The Ray of Hope	Howard D. Smiley	The Live Wire
Sep.	Many a Tear	M. P. Shiel	Pearson's Magazine
Sep.	The House of the Green Flame	George Allan England	The All-Story Magazine
Oct.	The Microbe of Fear	Charles S. Pearson	The Popular Magazine
1909			
Jan.	A Columbus of Space	Garrett P. Serviss	The All-Story Magazine 6
Mar.	The Land of the Lost	Roy Norton	The Popular Magazine 6
May	At His Mercy	Johnston McCulley	The Argosy 4
May	The Cataclysm	Stephen Chalmers	The All-Story Magazine 5
Jun.	My Time Annihilator	George Allan England	The All-Story Magazine
Sep.	The House of Transmutation	George Allan England	The Scrap Book 3
Oct.	A Hole Through the Earth	Camille Flammarion	Strand Magazine
Dec.	Beyond White Seas	George Allan England	The All-Story Magazine 6

"Around the World in 24 Hours"
by Stephen Cox, *The Argosy*, July
1910

"The Laughing Death" by Paul
D'Aydi, *All-Story Cavalier Weekly*,
March 27, 1915

ISSUE	TITLE	AUTHOR(S)	MAGAZINE
1910			
Mar.	The Girl in the Tower	Fremont Rider	The Blue Book
Apr.	No Doubt About It	Robert Brown	Cosmopolitan Magazine
Apr.	The Hawkins Vacu-Ornament	Edgar Franklin	Cosmopolitan Magazine
Jul.	Around the World in 24 Hours	Stephen Cox	The Argosy
Jul.	The Unparalleled Invasion	Jack London	MacClure's Magazine
Aug.	Just Back from Mars	R. K. Carter	National Magazine 2
Aug.	The Thought-Reading Machine: Baiting an Emperor	Alfred Williams	Short Stories
Sep.	The Monkey Man	William T. Eldridge	The Argosy 5
Sep.	The Hawkins Improved Diving-Bell	Edgar Franklin	The Argosy
Oct. 10	The City of Dread	E. White	The Popular Magazine
Nov.	The Power King	Frances P. Elliott	The Argosy 5
Nov.	The Silent Sounds	Epes Sargent	The Argosy

ISSUE	TITLE	AUTHOR(S)	MAGAZINE

1911

Jan.	The Devil Machine	Alfred Williams	Short Stories
Jan.	The Keynote Vibrator	?	Short Stories
Mar.	Love and the Ages	Charles D. Cameron	The Blue Book
Mar. 18	The Man in the Bottle	Victor Rousseau	Harper's Magazine
May	He of the Glass Heart	George Allan England	The Cavalier
Jul.	The Forest Reaper	William Eldridge	The All-Story Magazine 3
Jul.	Will-O'-The-Wisp	F. Comstock	The All-Story Magazine
Jul.	The Ribbon of Fate	George Allan England	The Cavalier
Jul.	The Second Deluge	Garrett P. Serviss	The Cavalier 7
Jul.	Samson in the Belfry	Charles B. Stilson	The Scrap Book
Aug.	The City of Gold	E. Bacon	The All-Story Magazine
Aug.	The Elixir of Hate	George Allan England	The Cavalier 4
Sep.	The Singing Devil	Buffington Phillips	The Cavalier
Nov.	The Person from the Pyramids	Perley Sheehan	Cosmopolitan Magazine

1912

Jan.	Darkness and Dawn	George Allan England	The Cavalier 4
Jan.	The Mind Master	Burton E. Stevenson	The Popular Magazine 6
Feb.	Under the Moons of Mars	Norman Bean (pseud. Edgar Rice Burroughs)	The All-Story Magazine 6
Feb. 17	The Occult Detector	J. U. Giesy & Junius B. Smith	The Cavalier 3
Mar.	Unsight-Unseen	William Tilinghast Eldridge	The All-Story Magazine 4
Mar. 9	The Significance of the High "D"	J. U. Giesy & Junius B. Smith	The Cavalier 3
May	A Flight to Freedom	E. Rath	Mystery Magazine
May 4	Voices of the Night	George Rodney	Short Stories
May 18	The Golden Blight	George Allan England	The Cavalier 6
Jun.	The Yap	E. Sargent & C. Jenkins	The All-Story Magazine
Jun.	The Luck Juice	Joe Ranson	The All-Story Magazine
Jun.	The Million Dollar Patch	George Allan England	The All-Story Magazine
Jun.1	The Wistaria Scarf	J. U. Giesy & Junius B. Smith	The Cavalier 3

ISSUE	TITLE	AUTHOR(S)	MAGAZINE
1912			
Aug. 10	In 2112	J. U. Giesy & Junius Smith	The Cavalier
Aug. 15	The Cloud-Bursters	Francis Lynde	The Popular Magazine 2
Oct.	Tarzan of the Apes	Edgar Rice Burroughs	The All-Story Magazine
Oct. 5	The Purple Light	J. U. Giesy & Junius Smith	The Cavalier 3
Nov.	Star-Dust	Stephen Chalmers	The All-Story Magazine 2
Nov.	The Selfrespectrometer	T. Bell	The All-Story Magazine
Nov. 1	The Flying Eye	Jacques Futrelle	The Popular Magazine

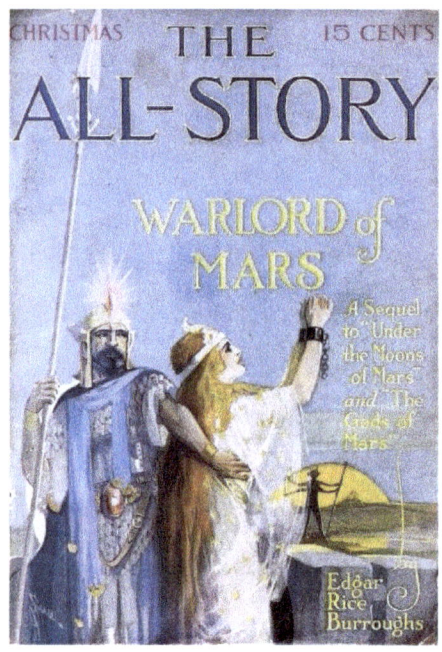 

"The Warlord of Mars" by Edgar Rice Burroughs, *The All-Story*, Dec. 1913

"Cloud Climbers" by Julian Hinckley, *All-Story Weekly*, March 28, 1914

ISSUE	TITLE	AUTHOR(S)	MAGAZINE

1913

ISSUE	TITLE	AUTHOR(S)	MAGAZINE
Jan.	The Gods of Mars	Edgar Rice Burroughs	The All-Story Magazine 5
Jan. 4	Beyond the Great Oblivion	George Allan England	The Cavalier 6
Jan. 11	Into the Fourth Dimension	Frank Blighton	Cosmopolitan Magazine
Jan 25	The Master Mind	J. U. Giesy & Junius Smith	The Cavalier
Feb.	The Crime Detector	George Allan England	The Cavalier
Mar.	Absolute Zero	Morgan Robertson	New Story
Apr.	The Poison Belt	A. Conan Doyle	Strand Magazine
Apr.	Hand O' God	Frank Condon	The Blue Book
Apr.	The Capture of New York	P. B. Malone	Century Magazine
May	The Destroyer	Burton E. Stevenson	The Popular Magazine 5
Jun. 1	The Battle Below Water	Edwin Balmer	The Popular Magazine
Jun. 14	Afterglow	George Allan England	The Cavalier 4
Jul.	The Cave Girl	Edgar Rice Burroughs	The All-Story Magazine 3
Jul. 5	The Mummy Case of Pharoah	William Holloway	Cosmopolitan Magazine
Jul. 5	Rubies of Doom	J. U. Giesy & Junius Smith	The Cavalier 2
Aug. 16	The Vengeance of Osiris	Hugh Pendexter	Cosmopolitan Magazine
Sep.	Inside Information	Charles Carey	The Argosy
Sep. 6	Birkholz's Molecular Theory	George Hulverson	Cosmopolitan Magazine
Oct. 1	The Biggest Story That Ever Happened	Henry W. Hyde	The Popular Magazine
Nov.	The House of Sorcery	Jack Harrower	The All-Story Magazine 4
Nov.	The Horror of the Heights	A. Conan Doyle	Everybody's Magazine
Nov.	A Man Without a Soul (aka The Monster Men)	Edgar Rice Burroughs	The All-Story Magazine
Nov. 15	The Seal Maiden	Victor Rousseau	The Cavalier
Dec.	The 'V' Force	Fred Smale	Short Stories
Dec.	The Horror	S. B. H. Hurst	Short Stories
Dec.	An Experiment	Alexander Crawford	Short Stories
Dec.	The Warlord of Mars	Edgar Rice Burroughs	The All-Story Magazine 4

ISSUE	TITLE	AUTHOR(S)	MAGAZINE
1914			
Jan.	Arovad the Terrible	De Casseres	Forum
Jan.	A Trap to Catch the Sun; A Prophetic Trilogy	H. G. Wells	Century Magazine
Jan.	The Woman from Yonder	Stephen F. Whitman	Century Magazine
Feb.	The Last War in the World (aka The World Set Free)	H. G. Wells	Century Magazine 2
Feb. 21	All for His Country	J. U. Giesy	The Cavalier 4
Feb. 23	The Millenium Engine	Levitt A. Knight	The Popular Magazine
Mar. 7	The Eternal Lover	Edgar Rice Burroughs	All-Story Weekly
Apr.	A Jungle Convert	Frederick Simpich	The Argosy
Apr. 4	At the Earth's Core	Edgar Rice Burroughs	All-Story Weekly 4
Jun. 20	The Frozen Beauty	Stephen Chalmers	All-Story Cavalier Weekly 3
Jun. 23	Beyond the Threshold	Joseph Ernest	The Popular Magazine
Aug. 8	In the Professor's Room	Redfield Ingalls	All-Story Cavalier Weekly
Sep. 26	My Friend Peterssen	James B. Hendryx	All-Story Cavalier Weekly
Oct. 10	The Lost Echo	Frank O'Brien	All-Story Cavalier Weekly
Nov. 14	The Empire in the Air	George Allan England	All-Story Cavalier Weekly 4
Dec. 5	The Fighting Soul	E. Franklin & G. Riddell	All-Story Cavalier Weekly

"Thuvia, Maid of Mars" by Edgar
Rice Burroughs, *All-Story Weekly*,
April 8, 1916

"At the Earth's Core" by Edgar
Rice Burroughs, *All-Story Weekly*,
April 4, 1914

ISSUE	TITLE	AUTHOR(S)	MAGAZINE
1915			
Jan.	Last Phase of the Great War: the German Invasion of America	?	American Magazine
Jan. 23	Sweetheart Primeval	Edgar Rice Burroughs	All-Story Cavalier Weekly 4
Feb.	Visions to Order	Lowell Hardy	The Argosy
Feb. 6	Judith of Babylon	Perley Poore Sheehan	All-Story Cavalier Weekly 5
Mar.	Out of the Shades	E. Williamson	The Argosy
Mar. 27	The Laughing Death	Paul D'Aydi	All-Story Cavalier Weekly 4
Apr. 7	Across a Million Years	George C. Shedd	The Popular Magazine
Apr. 23	The Inert Atom	Francis Lynde	The Popular Magazine
May	The Conquest of America in 1921	C. Moffett	MacClure's 4
May	The Moon Maiden	Garrett P. Serviss	The Argosy
May 1	Pellucidar	Edgar Rice Burroughs	All-Story Cavalier Weekly 4

ISSUE	TITLE	AUTHOR(S)	MAGAZINE
1915			
May 8	Abu the Dawn-Maker	Perley Poore Sheehan	All-Story Cavalier Weekly 6
May 15	The Tell-Tale Mirror	Helen E. Haskell	All-Story Weekly
May 22	The Unknown Quantity	Joseph Hazard	All-Story Weekly
May 22	The Old Exterminator	Edgar White	All-Story Weekly
Jul.	Hawkins-Heat	Edgar Franklin	The Argosy
Jul. 3	Indigestible Dog Biscuits	J. U. Giesy	All-Story Weekly
Sep. 4	The Fatal Gift	George Allan England	All-Story Weekly 4
Oct.	Saving the Nation	Cleveland Moffett	MacClure's Magazine 5
Nov. 6	X-Ray Eyes	A. deFord Pithey	All-Story Weekly
Dec. 11	Snared	J. U. Giesy & Junius Smith	All-Story Weekly 3
Dec. 18	The Tenth Question	George Allan England	All-Story Weekly
Dec. 18	Polaris of the Snows	Charles B. Stilson	All-Story Weekly 3
1916			
Jan. 1	The Sea Demons	Victor Rousseau	All-Story Weekly 4
Jan. 22	The Secret	Gilbert Riddell	Cosmopolitan Magazine
Feb. 19	Who Was Andrew Warren	Gilbert Riddell	The Argosy
Apr.	The Plunge	George Allan England	Snappy Stories
Apr. 8	Thuvia, Maid of Mars	Edgar Rice Burroughs	All-Story Weekly 3
Apr. 22	June 6, 2016	George Allan England	Collier's Magazine
Jun. 3	Box 991	J. U. Giesy & Junius B. Smith	All-Story Weekly 3
Jul.	Garden of Dreams	J. U. Giesy	All Around Magazine
Aug.	The Buddha's Elephant	Allan Hankwood	All Around Magazine
Aug. 12	Minos of Sardanes	Charles B. Stilson	All-Story Weekly 3
Oct. 7	Almost Immortal	Austin Hall	All-Story Weekly

"The Sea Demons" by Victor
Rousseau, *All-Story Weekly*, Jan. 1
1916

"The Cosmic Courtship" by Julian
Hawthorne, *All-Story Weekly*, Nov.
24 1917

ISSUE	TITLE	AUTHOR(S)	MAGAZINE
1917			
Feb.	The Gold of the Hidalgo	William A. Wolf	All Around Magazine
Feb.	Moh and the Mylodon	J. Allan Dunn	All Around Magazine
Feb.	The Bowl of Baal	R. A. Bennett	All Around Magazine
Feb. 17	Bill Jenkins, Buccaneer	George Allan England	All-Story Weekly 5
Mar. 31	The Cave Man	Edgar Rice Burroughs	All-Story Weekly 4
May 7	The Annihilator	Walter Darbig	The Popular Magazine
Jun.	The Messiah of the Cylinder	Victor Rousseau	Everybody's Magazine 4
Jun. 16	The Powder of Midas	Ben Ames Williams	All-Story Weekly 4
Jun. 20	The Odor of the Musk	H. E. Haskell	The Popular Magazine
Jun. 30	The Rebel Soul	Austin Hall	All-Story Weekly
Jul. 28	Swords of Wax	Ben Ames Williams	All-Story Weekly
Jul. 14	The Terrible Three	Tod Robbins	All-Story Weekly
Aug. 11	Warned	John D. Swain	All-Story Weekly

ISSUE	TITLE	AUTHOR(S)	MAGAZINE
1917			
Aug. 18	The Demise of Professor Manried	Philip Fisher, Jr.	All-Story Weekly
Sep. 1	Throne of Chaos	J. F. B.	All-Story Weekly
Sep. 15	Polaris and the Goddess Glorian	Charles B. Stilson	All-Story Weekly 5
Oct. 6	The Soul Trap	Charles B. Stilson	All-Story Weekly
Oct. 20	As It Was in the Beginning	Olin Lyman	All-Story Weekly
Nov. 7	Over There	Henry C. Rowland	The Popular Magazine 2
Nov. 24	Through the Dragon Glass	A. Merritt	All-Story Weekly
Nov. 24	The Cosmic Courtship	Julian Hawthorne	All-Story Weekly 4
Dec. 8	That Haunting Thing	Achmed Abdullah	All-Story Weekly

"The Planeteer" by Homer Eon Flint, *All-Story Weekly*, Mar. 9 1918

"Palos of the Dog Star Pack" by J. U. Giesy, *All-Story Weekly*, Jul. 13 1918

"After a Million Years" by Garrett
Smith, *The Argosy*, Jan. 18 1919

"Into the Infinite" by Austin Hall,
All-Story Weekly, Apr. 12 1919

ISSUE	TITLE	AUTHOR(S)	MAGAZINE
1919			
Jan. 11	Cursed	George Allan England	All-Story Weekly 6
Jan. 18	After a Million Years	Garrett Smith	The Argosy 6
Jan. 25	Forbidden Fruit	John Swain	All-Story Weekly
Jan. 25	His Inner Self	Philip Fisher	All-Story Weekly
Feb. 15	The Conquest of the Moon Pool	A. Merritt	All-Story Weekly 6
Feb. 15	That Receding Brow	Max Brand	All-Story Weekly
Feb. 22	The Runaway Skyscraper	Murray Leinster	The Argosy
Mar. 15	The Girl in the Golden Atom	Ray Cummings	All-Story Weekly
Mar. 29	The Mind Machine	Michael Williams	All-Story Weekly
Apr. 5	The Living Portrait	Tod Robbins	All-Story Weekly
Apr. 12	Into the Infinite	Austin Hall	All-Story Weekly 6
May 10	The Lord of Death	Homer Eon Flint	All-Story Weekly
May 10	Yedra of the Painted Desert	Charles B. Stilson	All-Story Weekly
May 24	The Man Who was Afraid	Philip Fisher	All-Story Weekly

ISSUE	TITLE	AUTHOR(S)	MAGAZINE
1919			
Jun. 7	The Riddle of the Almarose	Leslie Ramon	All-Story Weekly
Jun. 7	Footprints in the Snow	Murray Leinster	All-Story Weekly
Jun. 21	Fires Rekindled	Julian Hawthorne	All-Story Weekly
Jul. 5	The Mouthpiece of Zitu	J. U. Giesy	All-Story Weekly 5
Jul. 15	A Thousand Degrees Below Zero	Murray Leinster	The Thrill Book
Jul. 26	The Strange Case of Lemuel Jenkins	Philip Fisher	All-Story Weekly
Aug.	The Black Flyer	Edgar Rice Burroughs	Red Book
Aug. 9	Three Lines of Old French	A. Merritt	All-Story Weekly
Aug. 15	The Heads of Cerberus	Francis Stevens	The Thrill Book
Aug. 16	The Queen of Life	Homer Eon Flint	All-Story Weekly
Sep.	The Radium Seekers	Frank Duprie	The Blue Book
Sep. 1	The Silver Menace	Murray Leinster	The Thrill Book 2
Sep. 13	The Race of the Giants	Huntley Gibbs	The Argosy
Sep. 13	The Yellow Emerald	Francis James	The Argosy
Sep. 13	The Man Who could not Believe	Blanche Theodore	All-Story Weekly
Sep. 20	The Glyphs	Roy Norton	The Popular Magazine
Oct. 4	The Man in the Moon	Homer Eon Flint	All-Story Weekly
Oct. 4	The Volcanologist	Philip Fisher	All-Story Weekly
Oct. 7	Ark Right	Frank W. Chase	The Popular Magazine
Oct. 11	Between Worlds	Garrett Smith	The Argosy 5
Oct. 18	The Other Man's Blood	Ray Cummings	All-Story Weekly
Oct. 18	The Whimpus	Tod Robbins	All-Story Weekly 2
Oct. 25	A Man Named Jones	Charles B. Stilson	All-Story Weekly 5
Nov.	The Serpent City	Edison Marshall	The Blue Book
Nov. 1	The Great Cold	Clyde B. Hough	All-Story Weekly
Nov. 15	The Last Man	E. S. Darmady	Living Age
Nov. 15	The Flying Legion	George Allan England	All-Story Weekly 6
Nov. 29	Zapt's Repulsive Paste	J. U. Giesy	All-Story Weekly
Dec. 13	The Man Who Saved the Earth	Austin Hall	All-Story Weekly
Dec. 20	The Passing of the Great Cold	Clyde B. Hough	All-Story Weekly

"The Conquest of the Moon Pool" by A. Merritt, *All-Story Weekly*, Feb. 15 1919

"The Metal Monster" by A. Merritt, *Argosy All-Story Weekly*, Aug. 7 1920

ISSUE	TITLE	AUTHOR(S)	MAGAZINE
1920			
Jan.	The Cloth of Madness	Seabury Quinn	Young's Magazine
Jan. 3	The Green Splotches	T. S. Stribling	Adventure Magazine
Jan. 3	The Ship of Silent Men	Philip M. Fisher	All-Story Weekly
Jan. 3	Fire	Clyde B. Hough	All-Story Weekly
Jan. 10	The Man Who Discovered Nothing	Ray Cummings	All-Story Weekly
Jan. 17	The Course of Cave Love	Clyde B. Hough	All-Story Weekly
Jan. 17	The Eye of Balamok	Victor Rousseau	All-Story Weekly 3
Jan. 17	The Call from Stateroom 37	Philip M. Fisher	All-Story Weekly
Jan. 17	The Torch	Jack Bechdolt	The Argosy 5
Jan. 20	Wildfire	L. H. Robbins	The Popular Magazine
Jan. 24	Without a Rehearsal	Frank Blighton	The Argosy
Jan. 24	The People of the Golden Atom	Ray Cummings	All-Story Weekly 6
Jan. 24	Blind Man's Bluff	J. U. Giesy	All-Story Weekly
Jan. 31	Wings against the Cave Walls	Clyde B. Hough	All-Story Weekly

ISSUE	TITLE	AUTHOR(S)	MAGAZINE

1920

ISSUE	TITLE	AUTHOR(S)	MAGAZINE
Jan. 31	The Son of the Red God	Paul L. Anderson	The Argosy
Feb. 14	A Newer Dawn	Clyde B. Hough	All-Story Weekly
Feb. 14	A Priest of Quiche	Francis James	The Argosy
Mar. 1	Phantom Hound	Walter A. Dwyer	Top-Notch
Mar. 3	The Second Fall	S. B. H. Hurst	Adventure Magazine
Mar. 6	Claimed	Francis Stevens	The Argosy 3
Mar. 6	The Lord of the Winged Death	Paul L. Anderson	The Argosy
Mar. 20	The Master of Black	Philip M. Fisher	All-Story Weekly
Mar. 27	Dr. Martone's Microscope	Charles B. Stilson	All-Story Weekly
Apr. 24	The Greater Miracle	Homer Eon Flint	All-Story Weekly
May	The Thought Girl	Ray Cummings	Live Stories 2
May 8	The Cave That Swims on the Water	Paul L. Anderson	The Argosy
Jun. 12	The Mad Planet	Murray Leinster	The Argosy
Jun. 19	The Light Machine	Ray Cummings	All-Story Weekly
Jun. 26	The Land of the Shadow People	Charles Stilson	All-Story Weekly 5
Jul. 10	The Big Idea	Ray Cummings	The Argosy
Jul. 17	Into his Work	Philip M. Fisher	All-Story Weekly
Jul. 17	The Master of Magic	Paul L. Anderson	The Argosy
Aug.	L'Atlantide	Pierre Benoit	Adventure Magazine
Aug. 7	The Metal Monster	A. Merritt	Argosy All-Story Weekly 8
Sept. 25	The Sky Woman	Charles B. Stilson	Argosy All-Story Weekly
Aug. 28	The Wings of the Snow	Paul L. Anderson	Argosy All-Story Weekly
Sep. 3	Wolves of the Air	Ranger Gull	Adventure Magazine
Sep. 25	The Sky Woman	Charles B. Stilson	Argosy All-Story Weekly
Dec. 11	Treasures of Tantalus	Garrett Smith	Argosy All-Story Weekly 5

1921

ISSUE	TITLE	AUTHOR(S)	MAGAZINE
Jan.	The Other Road	Ray Cummings	Live Stories
Jan. 1	The Time Professor	Ray Cummings	Argosy All-Story Weekly
Jan. 18	The City of Baal	Charles Beadle	Adventure Magazine
Feb. 12	The Spirit Photograph	Ray Cummings	Argosy All-Story Weekly
Feb. 20	The Yellow Planet	Francis Perry Elliott	The Popular Magazine
Mar. 19	Catalepsy	J. U. Giesy	Argosy All-Story Weekly
Apr. 2	The Red Dust	Murray Leinster	Argosy All-Story Weekly
Apr. 2	The Curious Case of Norton Hoorne	Ray Cummings	Argosy All-Story Weekly
Apr. 9	The Lost City of Gold	George Shedd	Argosy All-Story Weekly

ISSUE	TITLE	AUTHOR(S)	MAGAZINE
1921			
Apr. 16	Jason, Son of Jason	J. U. Giesy	Argosy All-Story Weekly 6
Apr. 23	Madame Tsetse	George Allan England	Argosy All-Story Weekly
Apr. 23	The Curative Fear	Charles B. Stilson	Argosy All-Story Weekly
Apr. 23	Moon Madness	Ray Cummings	Argosy All-Story Weekly
May	The Blot of Ink	J. B. Harris-Burland	The Blue Book
May 7	The Gravity Professor	Ray Cummings	Argosy All-Story Weekly
May 14	The Blind Spot	Austin Hall & Homer Eon Flint	Argosy All-Story Weekly 6
Jun. 4	Nerve	Murray Leinster	Argosy All-Story Weekly
Jul. 7	Treasure of the Tombs	F. B. Austin	Adventure Magazine
Jul. 20	The Thunder Maker	L. H. Robbins	The Popular Magazine 2
Jul. 20	The Radium Veil	John Collier	The Popular Magazine
Jul. 23	The Devolutionist	Homer Eon Flint	Argosy All-Story Weekly
Aug. 18	The Throwback	Ferdinand Berthoud	Adventure Magazine
Aug. 27	Coil of Circumstance	Jack Harrower	Argosy All-Story Weekly
Aug. 27	Raiders of the Air	F. Barton & H. Kelley	Argosy All-Story Weekly
Sep.	The Magic Pencil	Ray Cummings	Munsey's Magazine
Sep. 3	The Emancipatrix	Homer Eon Flint	Argosy All-Story Weekly
Sep. 3	People of the Fourth Dimension	Ferdinand Berthoud	Adventure Magazine
Oct. 8	The Efficiency Expert	Edgar Rice Burroughs	Argosy All-Story Weekly 4
Nov. 19	Two Bits for Barry	Will Greenfield	Argosy All-Story Weekly
Nov. 20	High Tension	J. H. Greene	The Popular Magazine
Dec.	The Phantom Auto	Stoddard Goodhue	Everybody's Magazine
Dec. 3	The Great Silencer	Bernard V. Murphy	Argosy All-Story Weekly

"The People of the Golden Atom" by Ray Cummings, *All-Story Weekly*, Jan. 24 1922

"The Fire People" by Ray Cummings, *Argosy All-Story Weekly*, Oct. 21 1922

ISSUE	TITLE	AUTHOR(S)	MAGAZINE
1922			
Jan.	Test Tube Necromancy	Stoddard Goodhue	Everybody's Magazine
Jan.	Drops of Death	George Allan England	Munsey's Magazine
Jan. 20	Body of Blynn Anderson	H. Hutchinson	The Popular Magazine
Feb.	The Magic Wheel	Stoddard Goodhue	Everybody's Magazine
Feb. 18	The Chessmen of Mars	Edgar Rice Burroughs	Argosy All-Story Weekly 7
Mar. 4	The Gold Bug Sweepstakes	Wolcott Beard	Argosy All-Story Weekly
May	The Spirit of the Beast	Alan Sullivan	Everybody's Magazine
May 13	Worlds Within Worlds	Philip M. Fisher	Argosy All-Story Weekly
Jun.	The Spirit of the Man	Alan Sullivan	Everybody's Magazine
Jun. 24	The Peppermint Test	Ray Cummings	Argosy All-Story Weekly
Jul.	The Ladder in the Jungle	Alan Sullivan	Everybody's Magazine
Jul. 15	Lights	Philip M. Fisher	Argosy All-Story Weekly
Aug. 5	The Devil of Western Sea	Philip M. Fisher	Argosy All-Story Weekly
Aug. 7	Brains	Alan Sullivan	The Popular Magazine
Sep. 7	The Splendor of Asia	L. Adams Beck	?

ISSUE	TITLE	AUTHOR(S)	MAGAZINE
1922			
Sep. 9	Cloud Hawk	Garrett Smith	Argosy All-Story Weekly
Oct. 21	The Fire People	Ray Cummings	Argosy All-Story Weekly 5
Nov.	Secret of the Unseen Hand	Leslie Bereford	Action
1923			
Jan. 20	The Missing Mondays	Homer Eon Flint	Argosy All-Story Weekly 2
Feb. 20	Out of the Deep Sea	Thomas McMorrow	The Popular Magazine
Apr. 7	From Time's Dawn	B. Wallis	Argosy All-Story Weekly
Apr. 21	A Bunch of Keys	Philip M. Fisher	Argosy All-Story Weekly
May 5	The Moon Maid	Edgar Rice Burroughs	Argosy All-Story Weekly 6
May 26	The Thought Machine	Ray Cummings	Argosy All-Story Weekly
Jun. 9	The New Sun	J. S. Fletcher	Argosy All-Story Weekly
Jul. 7	The Three-Eyed Man	Ray Cummings	Argosy All-Story Weekly
Sep. 8	The Face in the Abyss	A. Merritt	Argosy All-Story Weekly
Oct.	The Last Man on Earth	John Swain	Mystery Magazine
Oct. 27	Fungus Isle	Philip M. Fisher	Argosy All-Story Weekly
Nov.	Sunken Cities	D. Newton	Mystery Magazine
Dec. 10	The Voice of Kali	Sax Rohmer	Short Stories
Dec. 15	Out of the Moon	Homer Eon Flint	Argosy All-Story Weekly 4
?	The Pool of the Stone God	W. Fenimore (aka A. Merritt)	American Weekly

"The Moon Maid" by Edgar Rice Burroughs, *Argosy All-Story Weekly*, May 5 1923

"The Blind Spot" by Austin Hall and Homer Eon Flint, *Argosy All-Story Weekly*, May 14 1921

ISSUE	TITLE	AUTHOR(S)	MAGAZINE
1924			
Feb. 16	In the Near Future	Joseph Ivers Lawrence	Argosy All-Story Weekly
Mar. 22	Up From the Abyss	P. L. Anderson	Argosy All-Story Weekly
Apr. 19	Colossus of the Radio	Leslie Ramon	Argosy All-Story Weekly
May	Beyond the Pole	Philip M. Fisher	Mystery Magazine
Jun. 28	The Radio Man	Ralph Milne Farley	Argosy All-Story Weekly 4
Jul. 12	The Man Who Mastered Time	Ray Cummings	Argosy All-Story Weekly 5
Aug. 16	The Nameless Doom	Charles A. King	Argosy All-Story Weekly
Sep. 6	Tuned Out	R. King	Argosy All-Story Weekly 4
Sep. 15	Wreckers Mysterious	Albert Treynor	Top-Notch
Oct. 18	Leaping Death	B. Wallis	Argosy All-Story Weekly
Nov. 1	Murder Music	Douglas Newton	Flynn's Detective Weekly
Nov. 1	Hate that Would Not Die	Maurice Coons	Flynn's Detective Weekly

ISSUE	TITLE	AUTHOR(S)	MAGAZINE
1924			
Nov. 8	The Ship of Ishtar	A. Merritt	Argosy All-Story Weekly 6
Dec. 6	Aladdin A.D. 1924	A. Temple	Argosy All-Story Weekly
Dec. 27	The Gas War	P. Mille	Living Age
1925			
Jan. 17	When the War Gods Walk Again	F. B. Austin	The Saturday Evening Post
Feb.	The Subconscious Witness	Stodard Goodhue	Everybody's Magazine
Feb. 7	Cleopatra's Cup	Robert H. Rhode	The Popular Magazine
Feb. 21	The Moon Men	Edgar Rice Burroughs	Argosy All-Story Weekly 4
Mar.	Hypostasia	R. Barstow	Everybody's Magazine
Mar. 7	Terror by Night	Gladys E. Johnson	Flynn's Detective Weekly
Mar. 21	The Radio Beasts	Ralph Milne Farley	Argosy All-Story Weekly 4
Apr. 11	The Tiger Weed	B. Wallis	Argosy All-Story Weekly
Jun. 6	The Silent Menace	Robert Russell	Flynn's Detective Weekly
Jun. 27	The Lightning Flash	Charles Rodda	Flynn's Detective Weekly
Sep. 5	The Red Hawk	Edgar Rice Burroughs	Argosy All-Story Weekly 3
Oct. 10	Creatures of the Ray	James L. Aton	Argosy All-Story Weekly
Oct. 20	The Town in the Sea	H. deVere Stacpoole	The Popular Magazine
Nov. 21	The Sun Makers	Will McMorrow	Argosy All-Story Weekly 3

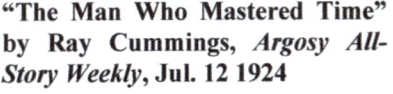

"The Man Who Mastered Time" by Ray Cummings, *Argosy All-Story Weekly*, Jul. 12 1924

"The Future Eve" by Julian Hawthorne, *Argosy All-Story Weekly*, Dec. 18 1926

ISSUE	TITLE	AUTHOR(S)	MAGAZINE
1926			
Jan.	The Black Star	George L. Knapp	The Blue Book
Jan. 9	The Vanishing Professor	Fred MacIsaac	Argosy All-Story Weekly 6
Jan. 16	The Trampling Horde	Paul Anderson	Argosy All-Story Weekly
Mar. 6	Wave Madness	Douglas Newton	Flynn's Detective Weekly
Mar. 20	Brethren of the Lamp	Howard Fitalan	The Popular Magazine
Apr. 8	Christ in Chicago	T. S. Stribling	Argosy All-Story Weekly
May 7	The Goddess from the Shades	John Buchan	The Popular Magazine 4
May 15	The Puppet	Gaston Leroux	Flynn's Detective Weekly 4
May 15	The Thing that Hunts in the Night	Marshall South	Argosy All-Story Weekly
Jun. 12	The Machine to Kill	Gaston Leroux	Flynn's Detective Weekly 4
Jun. 19	The Unknown Element	M. J. Phillips	Argosy All-Story Weekly
Jun. 26	The Genius Epidemic	John Wilstach	Argosy All-Story Weekly

ISSUE	TITLE	AUTHOR(S)	MAGAZINE

1926

Jun. 26	The Radio Planet	Ralph Milne Farley	Argosy All-Story Weekly 5
Jul. 3	The Great Commander	Fred MacIsaac	Argosy All-Story Weekly 4
Aug.	The Lord of the Mist	A. Conan Doyle	Canadian Magazine 12
Oct.	Child or Demon – Which?	Victor Rousseau	Ghost Stories
Dec. 18	The Future Eve	Comte Villiers d'Isle Adam	Argosy All-Story Weekly 6

1927

Jan.	The Doll that Came to Life	Victor Rousseau	Ghost Stories
Jan.	The Eye of Caesar	John D. Swain	Zest
Mar.	The Ghost of the Red Cavalier	Victor Rousseau	Ghost Stories
Mar. 27	The Last Judgment	J. B. S. Haldane	Harper's Magazine
Apr. 16	The World in the Balance	James Marshall	Argosy All-Story Weekly
May 7	The Lost Road to Yesterday	Garrett Smith	Argosy All-Story Weekly
Jun.	Rishi's Finger	G. Cross	Golden Book
Jun.	Fire—Water—and What?	Victor Rousseau	Ghost Stories
Jul.	The War Against the Moon	Andre Maurois	Forum
Jul.	When Manhattan Sank	George S. Brooks	Cosmopolitan Magazine
Jul. 2	Seven Footprints to Satan	A. Merritt	Argosy All-Story Weekly 6
Jul. 9	Venus or Earth?	Will McMorrow	Argosy All-Story Weekly
Jul. 16	Scourge of the Seven Seas	Garrett Smith	Argosy All-Story Weekly
Aug.	The Soul that Lost its Way	Victor Rousseau	Ghost Stories
Aug. 13	The Despised Comet	Garrett Smith	Argosy All-Story Weekly
Sep. 3	Going Down!	W. E. Parkhurst & W. B. Seabrook	Argosy All-Story Weekly
Oct. 1	The Flying Ghost	John Ames	Flynn's Detective Weekly
Oct. 8	The Maracot Deep	A. Conan Doyle	The Saturday Evening Post 4
Oct. 15	The Return of George Washington	George F. Worts	Argosy All-Story Weekly 6
Oct. 22	The Black Box of Silence	Francis Lynde	Popular Stories

ISSUE	TITLE	AUTHOR(S)	MAGAZINE

1927

Dec.	The House of the Living Dead	Victor Rousseau	Ghost Stories 6
Dec. 17	A World of Indexed Numbers	Will McMorrow	Argosy All-Story Weekly
Dec. 17	The Last Atlantide	Fred MacIsaac	Popular Stories 6

"The Radio Planet" by Ralph Milne Farley, *Argosy All-Story Weekly*, Jun. 26 1926

"The Princess of the Atom" by Ray Cummings, *Argosy All-Story Weekly*, Sep. 14 1929

1928

Jan.	The Blood Red Haze of Madness	W. H. Osborne	Secret Service
Jan.	The Death Trap	George Daulton	Secret Service
Jan. 7	Luckett of the Moon	Slater LaMaster	Argosy All-Story Weekly 4
Jan. 21	Slaves of the Wire	Garrett Smith	Argosy All-Story Weekly
Feb.	Coil of Circumstance	Jack Harrower	Secret Service 2
Feb. 11	Beyond the Stars	Ray Cummings	Argosy All-Story Weekly 3

ISSUE	TITLE	AUTHOR(S)	MAGAZINE
1928			
Feb. 26	Heroes of Science	Allan Saunders	Flynn's Detective Weekly
Mar.	The Dark Disk	Victor Rousseau	Cosmopolitan Magazine
Mar. 26	Gold and White Beauties	Douglas Newton	Flynn's Detective Weekly
Apr.	Doom!	Ray Cummings	Mystery Stories
Apr. 2	The Sapphire Flame	Douglas Newton	Flynn's Detective Weekly
Apr. 9	Into the Night Air	Douglas Newton	Flynn's Detective Weekly
Apr. 16	Reduced to Ashes	Douglas Newton	Flynn's Detective Weekly
Apr. 23	The Man Who Talked	Douglas Newton	Flynn's Detective Weekly
Apr. 30	The City of Tomorrow	Douglas Newton	Flynn's Detective Weekly
May	The Brain Master	Hamilton Thompson	Secret Service 3
May 12	In the Year 2000	Arthur O. Friel	Argosy All-Story Weekly 3
Jun.	The Master Ray	Eric von Kortlandt	Air Adventures
Jun.	Concerning Pliny Bolton	Wolton L. Beard	Mystery Stories
Jun.	The End of the World	E. J. Coatsworth	Dial
Jun. 30	World Brigands	Fred MacIsaac	Argosy All-Story Weekly
Jul.	The Man Who Caught the Weather	Bess Aldrich	?
Jul. 7	You've Killed Privacy!	Garrett Smith	Argosy All-Story Weekly
Jul. 7	The Vanishing Point	Francis Lynde	The Popular
Aug. 25	The Invisible Enemy	Cyril Berger	?
Sep. 8	Madman's Bluff	Will McMorrow	Argosy All-Story Weekly
Sep. 22	A Brand New World	Ray Cummings	Argosy All-Story Weekly 6
Oct.	The Winged Master	Fred Kaye	Wings
Oct. 20	Rain Magic	Erle Stanley Gardner	Argosy All-Story Weekly
Nov. 3	Thirty Years Late	Garrett Smith	Argosy All-Story Weekly 2
Dec. 1	The Girl in the Moon	Garrett Smith	Argosy All-Story Weekly 2

"The Girl in the Moon" by Garret Smith, *Argosy All-Story Weekly*, Dec. 1 1928

"Beyond the Stars" by Ray Cummings, *Argosy All-Story Weekly*, Feb. 11 1928

ISSUE	TITLE	AUTHOR(S)	MAGAZINE
1929			
Feb.	The Roselyn Experiment	J. W. Hammond	Youth's Companion
Mar.	Tanar of Pellucidar	Edgar Rice Burroughs	Blue Book 6
Mar. 2	The Sea Girl	Ray Cummings	Argosy All-Story Weekly 6
May	The Empire of the Arctic	Forbes Parkhill	The Blue Book
May 2	The Dark Ray of Death	F. N. Litten	Top-Notch
May 11	The Radio Flyers	Ralph Milne Farley	Argosy All-Story Weekly 5
Jun.	A Leap to Mars	L. Elwyn Backus	Aviation Mechanics 6
Jun.	The Flying Ship	Guy Fowler	Flying Stories 4
Jun. 22	The Shadow Girl	Ray Cummings	Argosy All-Story Weekly 4
Jul. 20	The Planet of Peril	Otis Adelbert Kline	Argosy All-Story Weekly 6
Aug.	The Man Who Rode the Lightning	Wulf Gray	The Blue Book
Aug.	In Twenty Twenty-Nine	Earl of Birkenhead	Century Magazine

ISSUE	TITLE	AUTHOR(S)	MAGAZINE
1929			
Aug.	The Prisoner of Life	Victor Rousseau	Ghost Stories 6
Sep.	Tarzan at the Earth's Core	Edgar Rice Burroughs	Blue Book 7
Sep. 14	The Princess of the Atom	Ray Cummings	Argosy All-Story Weekly 6
Oct. 1	The Headless Monarch	F. N. Litten	Top-Notch
Nov.	Haunted Airways	Thomson Burtis	American Boy 4
Nov.	Eight, Sixty-Seven	David H. Keller	Ten Story Book
Nov. 2	The Snow Girl	Ray Cummings	Argosy 4
Nov. 2	The Sky Octopus	Roy Norton	The Popular Magazine
Nov. 23	Our Distant Cousins	Lord Dunsany	The Saturday Evening Post
Nov. 30	The Darkness on Fifth Avenue	Murray Leinster	Argosy
Dec.	A 1950 Marriage	Amy Worth (pseud. of David H. Keller)	Paris Nights
Dec. 7	The Sky's the Limit	Erle Stanley Gardner	Argosy 2
Dec. 21	Maza of the Moon	Otis Adelbert Kline	Argosy 4
Dec. 28	The City of the Blind	Murray Leinster	Argosy

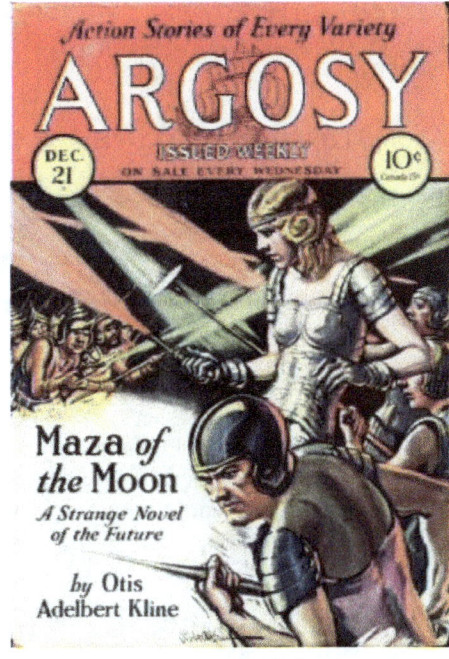

"The Sky's the Limit" by Erle
Stanley Gardner, *Argosy*, Dec. 7
1929

"Maza of the Moon" by Otis
Adelbert Kline, *Argosy*, Dec. 21
1929

ISSUE	TITLE	AUTHOR(S)	MAGAZINE
1930			
Feb. 1	The Earthquakers	Francis Lynde	The Popular Magazine
Feb. 8	The Man Who was Two Men	Ray Cummings	Argosy
Feb. 22	The Radio Gun-Runners	Ralph Milne Farley	Argosy 6
Mar.	Wings of Chaos	Arthur J. Burks	Flyers
Mar. 1	The Storm that Had to be Stopped	Murray Leinster	Argosy
Apr.	Back to Babylon	Bertram Atkey	The Blue Book
Apr.	A Fighting Man of Mars	Edgar Rice Burroughs	The Blue Book 6
Apr. 12	Sky Madness	Garrett Smith	Argosy
May	Say it with Clubs	Bertram Atkey	The Blue Book
Jun.	Pirate's Choice	Bertram Atkey	The Blue Book
Jun. 7	The Radio Menace	Ralph Milne Farley	Argosy 6
Jun. 14	The Man Who Put Out the Sun	Murray Leinster	Argosy
Jul.	Roughing it in Rome	Bertram Atkey	The Blue Book

ISSUE	TITLE	AUTHOR(S)	MAGAZINE

1930

Jul. 12	Spawn of the Comet	Otis Adelbert Kline	Argosy
Jul. 19	A Year in a Day	Erle Stanley Gardner	Argosy
Jul. 26	The Beast Plants	H. Thompson Rich	Argosy
Aug.	Wild Work with William the Conqueror	Bertram Atkey	The Blue Book
Aug.	The Electric King	Lord Dunsany	Harper's Magazine
Aug. 2	The Prince of Peril	Otis Adelbert Kline	Argosy 6
Aug. 2	Morgo the Mighty	Sean O'Larkin	The Popular Magazine 4
Sep.	Private Assassin	Bertram Atkey	The Blue Book
Sep.	The End of England	Douglas Newton	Excitement
Sep.	The Red Gem of Courage	R. F. Starzl	Argosy
Oct.	Ambassador to Mars	Minna Feibleman	Top-Notch
Oct.	Enoch Soames	Max Beerbohm	Golden Book
Oct.	The Man Who Limped	Otis Adelbert Kline	Oriental Stories
Oct. 25	The Snake Mother	A. Merritt	Argosy 7
Dec.	The Last Deluge	Hugh Pendexter	Star
Dec. 1	Men from Space	Charles Willard Diffin	The Popular Magazine
Dec. 13	Tama of the Light Country	Ray Cummings	Argosy 3

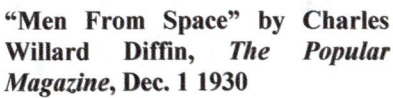

"Men From Space" by Charles
Willard Diffin, *The Popular
Magazine*, Dec. 1 1930

"The Snake Mother" by A.
Merritt, *Argosy*, Oct. 25 1930

ISSUE	TITLE	AUTHOR(S)	MAGAZINE
1931			
Jan.	Last Days of Atlantis	A. Noureddin Addis	Mystic World 4
Jan.	Death to America!	George F. Eliot	War Stories
Jan. 17	Caves of Ocean	Ralph Milne Farley	Argosy 4
Feb.	Above the Pole Star	John Miller Gregory	Man Stories
Feb.	The Land of No Shadow	Carl H. Claudy	American Boy
Feb.	Tires	H. F. Jamison	Mystic World 2
Mar.	The Weigher of Souls	Andre Maurois	Scribner's Magazine
Spring	The Dragoman's Secret	Otis Adelbert Kline	Oriental Stories
Apr.	The Mystery of the Black Box	?	Illustrated Detective Monthly
Apr.	Will It Ever Happen?	Capt. R. E. Dupuy	The Blue Book
May	The Flying Death	Hugh Pendexter	Star
May	Jungle Girl (aka The Land of Hidden Men)	Edgar Rice Burroughs	The Blue Book 5
Jun. 27	Tama, Princess of Mercury	Ray Cummings	Argosy 4

ISSUE	TITLE	AUTHOR(S)	MAGAZINE

1931

ISSUE	TITLE	AUTHOR(S)	MAGAZINE
Aug.	The Song of the Cakes	Nathan Schachner & Arthur Leo Zagat	Oriental Stories
Aug. 1	The Radio Pirates	Ralph Milne Farley	Argosy 4
Aug. 29	Bandits of the Cylinder	Ray Cummings	Argosy
Sep.	Nasturtia	Capt. S. P. Meek, USA	Strange Tales
Oct.	The War of 1941	Donald E. Keyhoe	Sky Birds
Oct. 3	Flyer of Eternal Midnight	Ray Cummings	Argosy
Oct. 31	The Jungle Rebellion	Ray Cummings	Argosy 6
Nov.	The Masterminds of Mars	Carl H. Claudy	American Boy 4
Nov.	The Black Mass	Capt. S. P. Meek, USA	Strange Tales
Dec.	Power Island	Peter van Dresser	Boy's Life 3
Nov.	When Dead Gods Wake	Victor Rousseau	Strange Tales of Mystery and Terror

"The Radio Pirates" by Ralph Milne Farley, *Argosy*, Aug. 1 1931

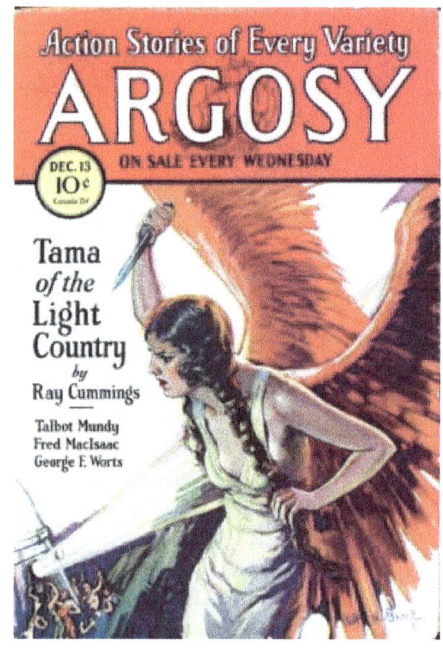

"Tama of the Light Country" by Ray Cummings, *Argosy*, Dec. 13 1930

ISSUE	TITLE	AUTHOR(S)	MAGAZINE
1932			
Jan.	Fintale the Merman	Bertram Atkey	The Blue Book
Jan.	The Smell	Francis Flagg	Strange Tales
Jan. 9	The Disappearance of William Roger	Ray Cummings	Argosy
Jan. 16	The Sleep Gas	Murray Leinster	Argosy
Jan. 23	Light of Atlantis	Sax Rohmer	Collier's Magazine
Jan. 23	Dwellers in the Mirage	A. Merritt	Argosy
Feb.	The Island of Life	J. B. Ryan	Popular Fiction
Feb.	The Queer Story of Brownlow's Newspaper	H. G. Wells	Ladies Home Journal
Feb. 20	M. Cliquant's Mistake	Douglas Newton	Liberty Magazine
Mar.	Spell of the Ghost	Henry Thompson	American Boy 4
Mar.	In the Name of Science	Milo Ray Phelps	Clues
Mar.	The Sinister Ray	Lester Dent	Detective Dragnet
Mar.	By the Hands of the Dead	Francis Flagg	Strange Tales
Apr. 16	The Insect Invasion	Ray Cummings	Argosy 5
May	For Sale–Murder	Will Levinrew	Thrilling Detective
May	A Million Years Ago	Carl H. Claudy	American Boy
May 28	In the Midst of Death	Ben Ames Williams	Liberty
Sum.	The Hidden Monster	David H. Keller	Oriental Stories
Jun.	Jungle Joss	Paul Regard	Thrilling Adventures
Jul.	The Moon Gods	Sidney Gowing & Edgar Jepson	The Blue Book 2
Jul.	The Wall of Fire	John M. Kirkland	The Blue Book
Jul.	The Man Who Could Work Miracles	H. G. Wells	Golden Book
Jul. 2	The Radio War	Ralph Milne Farley	Argosy 5
Aug.	Kwa of the Jungle	Paul Regard	Thrilling Adventures
Aug.	Nightmare House	Sax Rohmer	Illustrated Detective Monthly
Aug. 6	Death by the Clock	Ray Cummings	Argosy
Aug. 13	The Spot of Life	Austin Hall	Argosy 5
Sep.	When Worlds Collide	Edwin Balmer & Philip Wylie	The Blue Book 6
Sep.	The Chamber of Skulls	Roy B. Hinds	Popular Fiction
Sep.	The Invisible Horde	Lester Dent	Detective Dragnet
Sep.	The Damned Thing	Steven Anderson	The Blue Book
Sep.	The White Giant	Paul Regard	Thrilling Adventures
Sep. 17	Pirates of Venus	Edgar Rice Burroughs	Argosy 7
Oct.	Too Many Ghosts	Frank Condon	Illustrated Detective Monthly
Dec. 24	Rats of the Harbor	Ray Cummings	Argosy 2

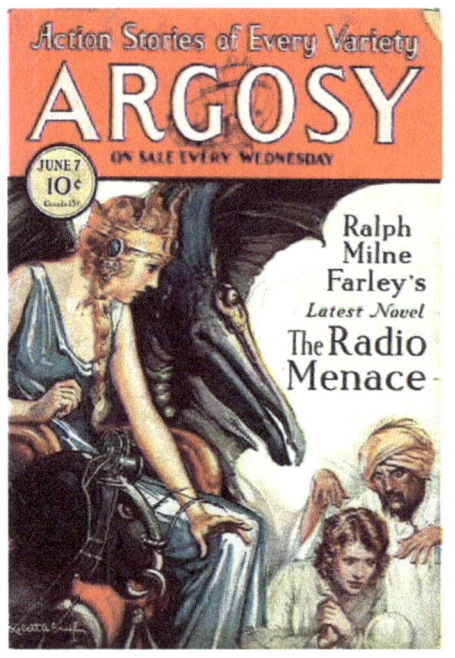

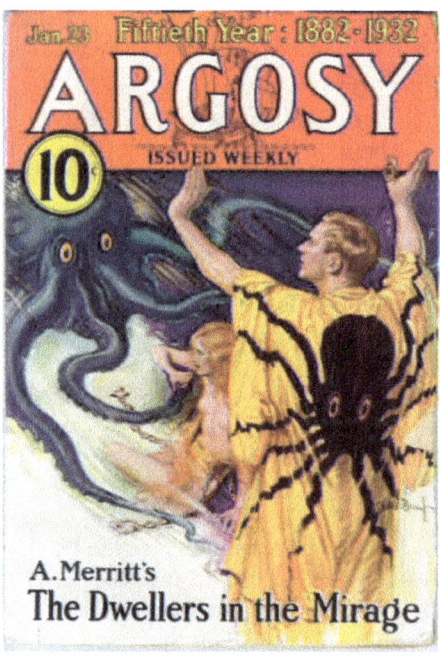

"The Radio Menace" by Ralph
Milne Farley, *Argosy*, Jun. 7 1930

"The Dwellers in the Mirage" by A.
Merritt, *Argosy*, Jan. 23 1932

ISSUE	TITLE	AUTHOR(S)	MAGAZINE
1933			
Jan.	The Crimson Blight	Arthur J. Burks	Thrilling Adventures 3
Jan.	The Mummy	John Wilstach	Mystery Magazine
Jan.	Great Circle	Peter van Dresser	Boy's Life 2
Mar.	Wings of Lucifer	Carl H. Claudy	American Boy
Mar.	King Kong	Walter F. Ripperger	Mystery Magazine
Mar. 4	Lost on Venus	Edgar Rice Burroughs	The Argosy 6
Apr.	No More a Corpse	Loring Brent	Novel-of-the-Month Magazine
Apr.	Kaldar, World of Antares	Edmond Hamilton	The Magic Carpet
Apr. 15	The Earth-Shaker	Murray Leinster	Argosy 4
May 13	The Golden City	Ralph Milne Farley	Argosy 6
Jun.	Stolen Battleships	Allan. K. Echols	Thrilling Adventures
Jun. 24	Finger of Doom	Garrett Smith	Argosy
Jul.	The Man Who was 63,000 Years Old	Jay Lucas	The Blue Book
Jul.	Valley of Giants	Jackson Cole	Thrilling Adventures
Jul. 8	World's End	Victor Rousseau	Argosy 3

ISSUE	TITLE	AUTHOR(S)	MAGAZINE
1933			
Jul. 26	Far as the Poles	Erle Stanley Gardner	Short Stories
Aug.	Skies of Doom	Frederick C. Painton	Thrilling Adventures
Aug. 19	The Lost Land of Atzlan	Fred MacIsaac	Argosy 6
Aug. 26	The Dragon's Power	Carl H. Claudy	The Classmate 12
Sep.	The Black Archangel	Michael Arlen	The Blue Book
Sep.	Zed Eight	A. Prestigiacomo	London Argosy
Sep.	The Queer Scarp	James Hopper	London Argosy
Sep. 23	The Fire Planet	Ray Cummings	Argosy 3
Oct.	Fangs of the East	Allan K. Echols	Thrilling Adventures
Oct.	The Snake-Men of Kaldar	Edmond Hamilton	The Magic Carpet
Nov.	After Worlds Collide	Edwin Balmer & Philip Wylie	The Blue Book 6
Nov. 4	Terror of the Unseen	Ray Cummings	Argosy
Nov. 25	The Outlaws of Mars	Otis Adelbert Kline	Argosy 7
Dec.	Pit of the God-Beasts	R. F. Starzl	Top-Notch

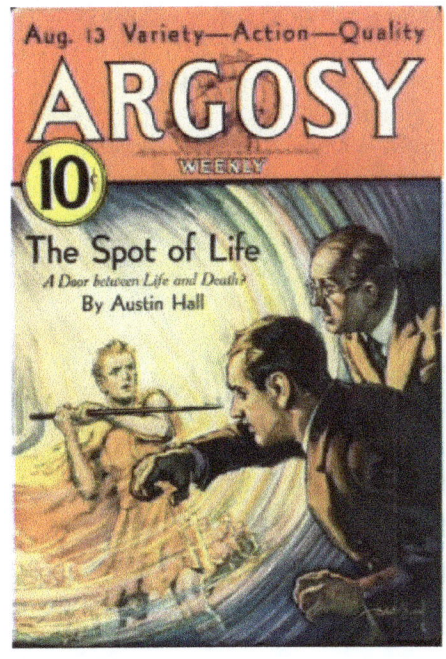

"The Spot of Life" by Austin Hall, *Argosy*, Aug. 13 1932

"The Outlaws of Mars" by Otis Adelbert Kline, *Argosy*, Nov. 25 1933

ISSUE	TITLE	AUTHOR(S)	MAGAZINE
1934			
Jan. 27	Brigands of the Unseen	Ray Cummings	Argosy
Feb.	The Metal Monster	John S. Endicott	Thrilling Detective
Feb.	Time Turns Back	Hal Field Leslie	Top-Notch
Feb.	Helmet of Pluto	Carl H. Claudy	American Boy
Feb.	It May be Tomorrow	George Bruce	Contact
Feb.	Son of Kong	?	Sure Fire Screen Stories
Feb.	The Radiant Enemies	R. F. Starzl	Argosy
Feb. 24	War of the Purple Gas	Murray Leinster	Argosy 2
Apr.	Blank Life	Nat Schachner	Clues
Apr.	The Dragon of Iskander	Nat Schachner	Top-Notch
May	A Clan is Born	J. H. Rosny	Top-Notch
May	The Robot Rebellion	Ray Cummings	The Blue Book
May 19	How Ryan Got Out of Russia	Lord Dunsany	Collier's Magazine
Jun.	The Day of the Dragon	Guy Endore	The Blue Book
Jul.	Forest of Fear	Charles Willard Diffin	Top-Notch
Jul. 28	Flood	Ray Cummings	Argosy 3
Aug.	The Man Who Bombed the World	S. Andrew Wood	The Blue Book 4
Aug.	Conquerors From the Stars	John T. McIntyre	Pictorial Review 5
Aug.	The Gray Death	Kenneth D. Whipple	Complete Detective Novel
Aug. 18	The Man Who Saved the World	E. Oppenheim	Collier's Magazine
Sep.	Shadow of Atlantis	Hal Field Leslie	Top-Notch
Sep.	Flight of the Conquistador	George Bruce	Squadron Magazine
Sep.	The Drone Man	A. Merritt	Fantasy Magazine (fan publication)
Oct.	Man of the Dawn	Charles Willard Diffin	Top-Notch
Oct.	The X Mystery	Charles H. Claudy	American Boy
Oct. 20	Earth-Mars Voyage 20	Ray Cummings	Argosy
Nov.	The Brain Snatcher	Dion de Jurnel	True Gang Life
Nov.	The Parachute Murders	Ralph Milne Farley & Al D. Nelson	True Gang Life
Nov.	Swords of Mars	Edgar Rice Burroughs	The Blue Book 6
Dec.	The Annihilator	Kenneth Robeson	Doc Savage
Dec.	Borderland	Arthur J. Burks	Thrilling Adventures
Dec.	A Million Years Hence	Carl H. Claudy	American Boy

ISSUE	TITLE	AUTHOR(S)	MAGAZINE

1934

| Dec. 25 | The Robot's Choice | Leslie Bernard | Detective Story Mag. |
| Dec. 29 | The Rollers | Murray Leinster | Argosy |

"The Fire Planet" by Ray Cummings, *Argosy*, Sep. 23 1933

"War of the Purple Gas" by Murray Leinster, *Argosy*, Feb. 24 1934

1935

Jan.	World of Doom	Ray Cummings	Thrilling Adventures
Jan.	Heritage	E. J. Derringer	Top-Notch
Jan.	The White Death	Robert Sydney Bowen	Dusty Ayres
Jan.	Deputy of the Devil	Ben Ames Williams	Red Book
Jan.	The X-Ray Eye	Robert J. Hogan	G-8 and his Battle Aces
Feb.	The League of War Monsters	Curtis Steele	Operator No.5
Feb.	Craig Kennedy Strikes Back	Arthur B. Reeve	Popular Detective
Feb.	Sublevel 17	Paul Ernst	Thrilling Adventures
Feb.	The Walking Cadaver	Maurice Renard	Top-Notch

ISSUE	TITLE	AUTHOR(S)	MAGAZINE
1935			
Feb.	Blue, Man of Thor	Clifton B. Kruse	Top-Notch
Mar.	O'Leary Fights the Golden Ray	Carson Mowre (editor)	Terence X. O'Leary's War Birds
Feb. 16	The Moon Plot	Ray Cummings	Argosy
?	Drugs of Doom	Ray Cummings	Thrilling Adventures
Mar.	The Dark Planet	John M. Reynolds	Boy's Life 4
Mar.	Outbound to Jupiter	Peter van Dresser	American Boy
Mar. 9	The Fang of Amm Jemel	Otis Adelbert Kline	Argosy
Apr. 13	The Polar Light	Ray Cummings	Argosy
May	The Swift Beast	Carl H. Claudy	American Boy
May	The Feast of Rah	Charles Willard Diffin	Top-Notch
May	The Murder Room	Otis Adelbert Kline	New Detective
Jun.	The Last Man on Earth	George F. Worts	Home
Jul. 6	Crimes of the Year 2000 -1	Ray Cummings	Detective Fiction Weekly
Jul. 19	The Ape Men of Vau	Morgan Farrell	Young America
Jul. 20	Crimes of the Year 2000 -2: The Television Alibi	Ray Cummings	Detective Fiction Weekly
Aug.	The Man who Met Himself	Ralph Milne Farley	Top-Notch
Aug.	Maid of the Moon	Kingsley Moses	The Blue Book
Aug.	Pachydermo	E. G. Wheeler	The Blue Book
Aug. 3	Crimes of the Year 2000 -3: Death in the Fog Tower	Ray Cummings	Detective Fiction Weekly
Aug. 10	The Morrison Monument	Murray Leinster	Argosy
Sep.	The Ultimate Adventure	Charles Willard Diffin	Top-Notch
Sep.	Fiend of the Hydrosphere	H. B. Moffett	Mystery Adventure
Sep.	The Underground Fiend	E. A. Willard	Mystery Adventure
Oct.	The Mist	David H. Keller	The Galleon
Nov. 30	The Extra Intelligence	Murray Leinster	Argosy
1936			
Apr.	The Earth Dwellers	Edmond Hamilton	Thrilling Mystery
May	Beasts that Once were Men	Edmond Hamilton	Thrilling Mystery
Aug. 15	Buccaneers International	Arthur H. Carhart	Argosy 3
Sep.	Khilit	Murray Leinster	Smashing Novels
Sep.	Death's Cold Daughter	Jack Williamson	Thrilling Mystery
Sep.	Children of Terror	Edmond Hamilton	Thrilling Mystery
Oct. 10	Space Station No. 1	Manly Wade Wellman	Argosy

ISSUE	TITLE	AUTHOR(S)	MAGAZINE
1936			
Dec.	Footprints in the Snow	Murray Leinster	Complete North-West Novel Magazine
Dec	The Stain that Grew	John Russell Fearn	Thrilling Mystery

WATCH FOR UPCOMING TITLES

IN THE S.F. HERITAGE SERIES!

About the Author

Igor Spajic has read science fiction all his life, with an increasing interest in the earlier years of the genre. Apart from the pulp magazine era of the 1920s through the 1940s, Igor has discovered a rich vein of works written before even the term 'science fiction' was coined.

If you have suggestions for the revival of classic writing and artwork from illustrated novels of science fiction or fantasy, you can contact Igor at:

flashpointgrafx@optusnet.com.au

www.ingramcontent.com/pod-product-compliance
Lightning Source LLC
Chambersburg PA
CBHW070418120726
47909CB00005B/1704